HYPNOSIS

A TALE OF MYSTERIOUS FEMINIZATION

NIKKI CRESCENT

HONEY HUT PUBLISHING

NEWSLETTER

KEEPING UP WITH NIKKI CRESCENT

JOIN NIKKI CRESCENT'S MAILING LIST!

Thank you for picking up one of my books! Chances are I'm in the process of working on another one! Hey—Did you know that you can read my whole catalogue free if you subscribe to **Kindle Unlimited**? It's true! If you aren't subscribed, I would highly recommend it.

I have started this little newsletter to let all of my beautiful readers know when I'm offering discounts, releasing new books, and giving away **EXCLUSIVE CONTENT FOR FREE**. The sign up takes about four seconds (seriously). I will never share your email address with anyone, you will never receive any spam, and you can unsubscribe at any time with the click of a single button.

COPYRIGHT

COPYRIGHT INFORMATION

FIND ME ON PATREON!

I really hope that you're enjoying my work! I've been fortunate enough to make this my full-time job for the past couple of years, though it hasn't been easy. There's a lot of financial uncertainty as a full-time self-published writer.

I would feel tremendously blessed if you would venture on over to my Patreon page and consider supporting me there. I think you will be excited by what I have to offer: **a community, free book chapters, pictures, contests, commissions, free stories, advanced releases, and much more**. It's the only way to get your hands on these exclusive titles:

THE PUNISHMENT
FORCED

TWINS
LORI'S LAST FUCK
THE GIRL TWIN (A Full-Length Novel)
TRANS CAM WHORE
GETTING READY FOR PROM
DUBIOUS CONSENT
PETRA'S FRISKY PHOTOSHOOT
JILLIAN'S 14 INCHES
THREE WISHES
HIS BIGGEST FAN
TRUTH OR DARE
ONLY GIRLS GET A RIDE
WEREWOMAN

And for as little as a dollar per month—is that even a
quarter cup of Starbucks coffee?
Be the gorgeous, filthy doll you know that you are
and come hang out with me:

https://www.patreon.com/nikkicrescent

DEDICATION

To the real Dr. Lee

If only, if only...

;)

Love,
Nikki Crescent

HYPNOSIS

Owen Baker has tried everything to quit smoking—
everything except for hypnosis. His hopes aren't
high when he goes into Dr. Sandra Lee's office, but
he's willing to try anything. Dr. Lee is supposedly
the best in the business, after all.

The session is short, lasting only five minutes,
but amazingly, Owen seems to be cured. His urges to
smoke don't return, and he suddenly has a new lease
on life…

But he can't help but notice a strange new problem: episodes of lightheadedness that always seem to
end with the intense urge to rest. He's experiencing
hours of lost time. And even stranger, people on the
streets are starting to recognize Owen, asking him
strange questions like, 'Why aren't you dolled up

today?' and making creepy comments like, 'Last night was a lot of fun.'

Maybe Owen has a female doppelgänger running around town... or maybe Dr. Lee did something sinister when she had Owen under her hypnotic trance.

I'd been on that waitlist for seven months. "We just had a cancellation. Can you make it in today?" the receptionist asked me over the phone.

"I'll be right there!" I said, springing to my feet.

Hypnosis was my last resort. I'd tried everything else: patches, vaping, dipping cigarettes into apple cider vinegar so that they would taste rancid when lit… I'd read all of the books on quitting, and I'd even had a few health scares that should have helped —but nothing worked. I would continue to get up in the morning, craving a cigarette, no matter how desperately I wanted to stop.

"Is it possible for you to be here in one hour?" asked the receptionist.

"No problem," I lied. The clinic was over an hour from my house, and now, I was still in my pyjamas. I was still in bed. I even wondered for a moment if I was still asleep, and this was all some sort of dream. It really did seem too good to be true, but I usually didn't have nice dreams; I was one of those people who only ever had nightmares.

I jumped out of bed and rushed to the bathroom to get ready. As I brushed my teeth, I looked at myself in the mirror. My clothes were outdated and ill-fitting, a stark reminder of my poor income... I'd been fired from my job at the recreation centre because my boss got sick of me showing up, smelling like cigarette smoke. Then, I got fired from my job at the daycare because I was caught smoking a cigarette outside, on the little playground (I made sure the wind was blowing the smoke away from the kids, of course).

The only job I was able to get was washing dishes at an old pub, making minimum-wage. Those damned cigarettes were holding me back from everything in life, it seemed...

Even my clothes took a hit. My once-white shirt was now a slight tone of yellow, and I couldn't help but wonder if that was from the cigarette smoke.

I sighed and decided to push those thoughts aside. Today was about quitting smoking, not worrying about my appearance.

After a quick shower, I walked over to my closet to pick out an outfit. I settled on a pair of faded jeans and a t-shirt, nothing too fancy. I hastily put on my shoes and grabbed my wallet and car keys. As I rushed out the door, I couldn't help but glance back at my small apartment.

It was a tiny one-bedroom apartment with a single window that faced the street. The paint on the walls was starting to peel, showing the blue that the previous tenant had made every single wall in the house. My furniture was old and worn out, and it probably smelled like cigarette smoke. But it was home, and I was grateful to have a roof over my head... I guess.

I hurriedly made my way to the car and drove off to my appointment. As I drove, I mentally prepared myself for the hypnosis session. I knew it wouldn't be easy, but I was determined to quit smoking for good. I will admit that I was a bit scared, not knowing what to expect. I didn't love the idea of relinquishing control to some therapist, letting her dabble around in my brain, picking through my thoughts. I didn't know much about hypnosis, but from the research I'd done online, I knew that a good hypnotherapist could make a patient say just about anything.

I liked to think of myself as a private person. I didn't often share details about my life with anyone. I couldn't help but wonder if the hypnosis would even work, or if I would be too guarded, to resistant, too scared to reveal the thoughts that I had stashed away in my head.

I arrived at the hypnotherapist's office, and as I stepped out of the car, I took a deep breath. This was it. I was ready to finally kick the habit.

I had one last smoke. I savoured it. "I'm not going to miss you," I whispered to that terrible stick of poison right after an unpleasant coughing fit. "I can't wait to throw all you little fuckers straight into the trash."

As I walked into the office, I felt a sense of calm wash over me.

Today was the day that everything would change.

I was struck by how different that clinic looked from any other doctor's office I had been to. The decor was hip, trendy, and modern, with sleek black and white furniture and abstract art on the walls. There was a strange statue of some African tribeswoman, doing some sort of strange dance.

"Hello there," said a soft voice across the room. She was sitting on a large yoga ball, with a tiny white desk in front of her. I guess she was the receptionist. "You must be Owen Baker." Her voice was so calm; I wondered if I'd walked into some cult meeting.

She greeted me with a warm smile and directed me to the waiting area. As I sat down on the plush couch, I noticed that there were no outdated magazines or medical pamphlets. Instead, there were interesting books and magazines on wellness, self-help, and personal growth.

The room had a pleasant aroma, a mix of lavender and eucalyptus. Soft instrumental music played in the background, adding to the peaceful atmosphere.

As I waited, I took in my surroundings. The hypnosis clinic had a peaceful and calming ambiance, which made me feel comfortable and at ease. The lighting was soft, and the decor had a minimalist feel, with a few carefully chosen pieces adding to the overall vibe.

The hypnotherapist came out to greet me, and I couldn't help but notice her stylish outfit and big, cult-like smile. She led me to a private room that had a comfortable recliner and soft blankets. The room was dimly lit, which added to the calming effect… at least, that's what it was supposed to do. In all honesty, they'd swung the pendulum way too far in that other direction, making me truly feel like I was about to be initiated into some strange cult. "Neat place," I said, looking around.

She didn't reply, just staring at me with that

weird smile. Then, after a long, silent moment, she said, "I want to tell you about hypnotherapy."

Dr. Lee, the hypnotherapist, explained the process and the benefits of hypnosis, and I was eager to start, to get it over with. She was an older broad, with wrinkles around her eyes and silver hair styled in a short bob. She wore a white lab coat, but it was her calm demeanour—or maybe I should say, her cult-leader demeanour—that caught my attention. Her blue eyes were clear, but her extreme calmness made me feel like I was being hypnotized just by being in her presence.

But I reminded myself that she was the best. She was world-renowned, with a stellar reputation that preceded her. Her name was spoken with reverence in the medical community, and patients from all over the world sought out her services. She had trained with some of the greatest minds in hypnotherapy and had developed her own unique approach that was both effective and highly sought after. Her reputation was built on years of experience and a proven track record of success in helping patients overcome their personal struggles...

At least that's what her website said... Maybe it was all bullshit. It's not like anybody looks into it. It's not like any normal person has ever heard of a 'Trance Master' award... In fact, when I first read it, it sounded like total rubbish... so I looked into it. Here's what the website said:

Introducing the "Trance-Master" award, an annual recognition given to the best hypnotherapist in the world. This prestigious award is presented to the hypnotherapist who has shown exceptional skill in the art of hypnotherapy and has made a significant impact on the field.

The Trance-Master award is the ultimate recognition in the hypnotherapy community, and it is highly sought after by both established and up-and-coming hypnothera-pists. It is awarded based on a variety of criteria, including the number of successful sessions, patient satis-faction, and contributions to the field of hypnotherapy.

The award is presented at an annual gala event,

which is attended by the top hypnotherapists in the world. The winner receives a trophy that is made of crystal and shaped like a pendulum, which symbolizes the hypnotic trance that they have mastered.

In addition to the trophy, the winner of the Trance-Master award is also given a significant monetary prize and is featured in various publications and media outlets. The winner's name is also added to a prestigious list of past winners, which includes some of the most respected and successful hypnotherapists in history.

The Trance-Master award is not only a recognition of the recipient's talent and skill, but it is also a celebration of the power of hypnotherapy to transform lives. The award serves to inspire and motivate hypnotherapists to continue to push the boundaries of the field and to help *more people achieve their goals through the power of hypnosis.*

Blah, blah, blah. I didn't care about what awards she'd won. I just wanted her to end my smoking habit. I was even willing to pay the $5,600 price tag for that ninety-minute session; that's how desperate I was.

Jimmy, my buddy, thought that I was insane when I told him how much I was paying. He thought I was a downright lunatic when I told him that results weren't guaranteed, and that there was no refund if the session failed.

But... I was desperate. So I got settled onto that black leather couch. I got into the position that she wanted me in. I took deep breaths when she told me to take deep breaths. I looked into her intense eyes every time she told me to look into her intense eyes.

She began to speak in a soft, soothing voice, "Owen, take a deep breath in and slowly release it. Let your body relax and sink into the chair. You are in a safe and comfortable place."

I found myself resisting the suggestion, feeling hesitant about letting go of control. My muscles tensed up, and I struggled to relax. I couldn't shake the feeling that I was being put under someone's spell.

"Imagine that you are walking down a path in the woods," she continued. "The path is peaceful, and the birds are chirping. You feel calm and relaxed. You are in control of your thoughts and feelings."

I tried to imagine the scene as she described it, but I couldn't fully immerse myself in the experience. I was too nervous and self-conscious, feeling like I was being tricked into doing something I didn't fully understand. I knew that I needed this... I knew that I needed to give in.

But I was so scared... scared of what she might find if she started poking around in my head.

"Now, imagine that you are holding a balloon in your hand," she said. "This balloon represents your addiction to smoking. You have the power to let go of the balloon and release the addiction. You can choose to be free from it."

As she spoke, I found myself becoming more hesitant. I couldn't fully let go of my addiction, feeling like it was a part of me that couldn't be easily discarded. I wanted to be free from it, but I didn't know if I was ready to take that step.

"No," I whispered. I was shocked that I said it out loud.

"Let it go, Owen," she said.

I bit down on my tongue.

"Take a deep breath in and slowly release it," she said. "When you open your eyes, you will feel calm and refreshed. You will be ready to face the world with a renewed sense of energy and purpose."

As she finished her statement, I opened my eyes, feeling like nothing had changed. I laughed and looked over at her, "Okay, so when are we doing the real thing?"

She smiled. "That was it," she said. "Thank you for coming in today. I hope that your life is better after today. In fact, I know it will be better."

"Wait… Are you fucking serious right now? That was what I paid six grand for!?"

"Your time is up," she said. "Be sure to come back in a month for your followup."

"Wait," I said, shaking my head. "That was not hypnosis. You just told me to imagine popping a balloon! I could have done that in bed. I drove halfway across the province for this!"

"I'm sorry, Owen," she said. "I'm sure that the receptionist explained the process to you over the phone when you booked your appointment." She turned up her chin and smiled, and in that instant, I realized that this whole thing was just a scam to rip off desperate people like me...

And worse! She was ripping off grieving people too. There was a woman in the waiting room bawling her eyes out because she'd miscarried a baby. How could someone seriously sleep at night after taking advantage of grieving mothers?

"You're a sick woman," I said to her, glaring into her eyes with a scowl on my face. I couldn't help it; I just couldn't stand what she was doing to people.

"I think you should see yourself out," she said, giving me an identical glare right back.

"I think you should have your license revoked," I growled.

"And why is that?" she asked, starting to tense up. It was the first time she didn't look quite so calm and tranquillized, as if whatever pot she smoked before I arrived had worn off.

"You're just taking people's money. I paid for ninety minutes, and I haven't even been here for five! Now you're saying I'm done!? You didn't do shit!"

"It doesn't always take a lot to get a desired result," she said slowly, as if she was explaining herself to a four-year-old. "Now leave, before I call security on you."

I stormed out of that building, hands clenched into tight fists. I was muttering swear words under my breath. The more I thought about it, the more I became convinced that the hypnotherapist was a fraud. How could anyone have the power to hypnotize someone so easily? It all seemed too good to be true. Did she really win that award? I looked up the award before the session... but maybe I should have tried to find some proof that she actually won it.

I drove through the streets of the rundown town. The heavy traffic and the chaos that seemed to dominate the city was particularly overwhelming. Cars were honking and weaving in and out of lanes, pedestrians were jaywalking and shouting, and the buildings on either side of the street looked especially old and decrepit, seemingly closing in on the streets, eating up lanes, forcing all of those cars into just a couple of congested lanes...

The streets were narrow, with potholes and cracks in the pavement. The buildings were rundown, with peeling paint and broken windows. The sidewalks were littered with trash and debris, and the air was thick with the smell of exhaust fumes. Someone honked at me, for seemingly no reason. I leaned out the window and shouted back at her. Then, she screamed at me and said, "You probably have a small cock, asshole!"

I still don't know what I'd done... dumb cow.

As I drove through the streets, I noticed the different businesses that lined the sidewalks. There were small mom-and-pop stores, fast-food restaurants, and check-cashing places. The signs on the buildings were faded and peeling, and the neon lights were flickering. A homeless man was taking a piss right on the road, with his pecker loosely flopping left and right as he ran his hands through his dirty hair. I looked away, disgusted and annoyed.

The people in the town seemed to be in a rush, hurrying to get where they needed to go. It was as if time was of the essence, and there was no room for slowing down or taking a moment to appreciate the world around them... though, to be fair, there wasn't much to appreciate in that lousy town.

As I pulled into my driveway, I felt a sense of disappointment. I had hoped that the hypnotherapy session would be the key to unlocking my potential and helping me overcome my addiction to smoking. But now, I was left feeling more confused and frustrated than ever.

I went inside and sat down on my couch, still brooding over what had just happened. I felt like I had wasted my time and money on a therapy session that was nothing more than a scam.

But as I sat there, I realized that I hadn't had a single cigarette since the session. It had been two hours—and I should clarify that they were two extremely frustrating hours.

And not once did I have the urge to smoke…

But surely now that I was thinking about cigarettes, I would want to grab one.

That urge never came. In fact, the thought of smoking was… off-putting.

Hold up… Did the hypnosis actually… work?

CHAPTER 2

*N*ight came. I still didn't have the urge to smoke. It was already a new record: six hours without a cigarette between my lips; I didn't even make it that far when I was chewing that gum.

Were the urges gone?

I thought for sure that I would wake up with one of those familiar urges. I usually had a smoke in the middle of the night (it was rare that I made it through eight hours of sleeping without waking up for a nicotine fix).

But there were no urges that morning.

Over the next few days, I began to notice a significant change in myself. The urges to smoke that had been a constant presence in my life for years were suddenly gone. I felt more energized and focused than I had in a long time.

I could breathe better, almost instantly.

At first, I was a bit skeptical. I couldn't believe that the hypnotherapy session had been so effective. But as the days passed, I became more and more convinced that the session had done exactly what it was supposed to do - break my addiction to smoking.

There was not one single urge to smoke.

I found that I had more time and energy than ever before. I was able to focus on my work and hobbies without the constant distraction of nicotine cravings. My sense of taste and smell had improved, and I felt more confident in my ability to stick to healthy habits.

I was amazed at how much my life had changed in just a few short days.

As the weeks and months passed, I continued to feel more and more like my old self - before I was a smoker. I had more energy, better focus, and a renewed sense of purpose. I knew that I had made the right decision to seek out the help of a hypnotherapist... Maybe I owed the woman an apology. I skipped out on the followup session, worried there would be a guard there to escort me away if I showed up.

I decided to send her a card. I went to the dollar store, picked out a nice thank-you card, and inside, I wrote, "I'm sorry for yelling at you." I mailed the card that day, and I will admit that it made me feel a little bit better about snapping at the old broad.

Yet I was confused, remembering back on that appointment, which only lasted five minutes. How was she able to break my addiction with so few words? She just told me to pop an imaginary balloon... that was it... and that was enough to make me quit a twenty-year addiction, cold-turkey, with no withdrawals whatsoever. It just seemed too good to be true.

I don't want to bore you with so many details,

but I do want to tell you how quickly my life improved.

I dropped off some resumes to find a new, better-paying job, and for the first time ever, I was well-received. I got a new job, making almost double what I made washing dishes. When I took the bus or the train, people didn't move away from me. In fact, strangers would start chatting with me. A young, pretty woman even started chatting with me one afternoon, and I left the train with her phone number.

I was smiling more often. I even started going to the gym, finally able to exercise for more than ten minutes without getting winded.

Life was great.

I had no complaints…

Until one day, as I was leaving the gym, a large, muscular man walked up to me with a grin on his face and said, "Don't feel like playing today?"

I stared at him for a moment. "Sorry?"

"We had fun yesterday," he said. "I'd love to do it again."

"Do what again?" I asked.

I searched my memory, but I couldn't place him. I shook my head and apologized, but he just laughed and said, "No worries, man. We had a good time, though, didn't we?"

I was sure that he was talking to the wrong person. Maybe I looked like someone else...

But it almost seemed like he was talking to a girl. Maybe he was guy—I'm not one to judge.

I didn't know what he was talking about, but his

tone made me feel uneasy. I looked at him more closely, taking in his appearance. He was wearing a tight-fitting tank top that showed off his muscular arms and a pair of gym shorts that hugged his thighs.

His skin was tanned and smooth, and his face was chiseled and handsome. He had a bit of stubble on his chin, and his hair was short and styled in a messy, just-out-of-bed look. He was a large, gym-toned man with bulging muscles and a stern expression on his face. He was the kind of guy who looked like he could bench-press a car and not break a sweat.

Despite his impressive physique and good looks, there was something about him that made me feel uneasy. The memory of our supposed time together was a complete blank to me, and I couldn't help but feel like there was something off about the whole situation.

I brushed that particular conversation off, but then, the very next day, something weird happened again. I was approached, in the street, by a thin man with a rough, homeless appearance. He winked at me and then he said, "No dress today? It's a shame; you looked so cute last week."

"Last week?" I said. "Dress? What are you on about?"

"Oh, sorry," he said, turning red. "I might have the wrong guy."

It was a quick encounter. The man scurried off, embarrassed, and I was just left feeling strange, and uncomfortable. I was starting to wonder if I had some doppelgänger running around town, flirting with men, wearing women's clothes. That's certainly how it seemed after it happened for a third time. I was walking down the street, minding my own business, when another stranger approached me. He was a tall, thin man with dark hair and an unsettling glint in his eye.

"Hey there, why aren't you dressed like a girl?" he asked, grinning at me. There was a certainly terrifying bluntness about that question.

I was taken aback by the question. He had the wrong person. "Excuse me?" I said, trying to keep my voice calm.

"You heard me," he said, getting closer to me. "You're supposed to be dressed like a girl, but you're not. What's the deal? You're normally dressed like a girl."

I shook my head, feeling confused and unnerved by the stranger's behaviour. "I have no idea what you're talking about. You've got the wrong person," I said, trying to walk away.

But the stranger didn't let me go. He kept following me, insisting that I was the one he was looking for. He was getting more and more agitated, and I could feel my heart rate starting to rise.

I tried to stay calm and rational, but the stranger's behaviour was becoming increasingly erratic. I didn't know what to do, and I started to feel like I was in danger.

Eventually, I was able to break free from the stranger and escape. I was shaken by the encounter, and I couldn't help but wonder what had set him off. It was a disturbing reminder that there are some truly unstable people out there...

But he was saying something that I was hearing more and more: men who were convinced that they'd seen me as a girl, or been with me as a girl.

It happened again a couple of days later. "Hey man, do you have a twin sister?" asked a man with a nervous grin. He was staring into my eyes. And this encounter was especially odd, because I was forty minutes from my home, running an errand in a rougher end of town.

"Someone asked me the same thing the other day," I said. "Why do people keep asking me the same thing?"

"There's a girl who looks just like you," he said. "I've seen her a few times down here. She's really... something."

"Something?" I said. "What does that mean? What does *something* mean?"

"I don't know," the man said. Then, he laughed. "She's, uh... outgoing. Let's just leave it at that."

"No," I said. "I don't want to leave it at that. People keep telling me about this girl. It's starting to get annoying."

"I don't know, man," the older fellow said. "She just comes through here sometimes, flirting with everyone she sees. She just... looks a lot like you. But, of course, she looks like a girl, and you're clearly not a girl."

I finished my errand, starting to feel more and more uneasy about this doppelgänger who had seemingly come out of nowhere. I tried to convince myself that it wasn't a big deal.

But it got weirder... a lot weirder.

I was walking down the street, lost in my thoughts, when a young woman approached me. She was tall and thin, with long red hair and a fierce expression on her face.

"You!" she shouted, pointing her finger at me. "You ruined my relationship! You stupid fucking whore!"

I was taken aback by her sudden outburst and couldn't help but feel confused. "What are you talking about?" I asked, trying to keep my voice calm.

"You know exactly what I'm talking about!" she said, getting closer to me. "You were the one who came between us, and now he's gone! You think you can just get dressed up like a girl and seduce guys… It's fucking weird! And you should be ashamed!"

Now, people were turning to look. I felt my skin turning red. I had no idea what this woman was on about.

I shook my head, feeling more and more bewildered by the moment. I had no idea what she was talking about, and I couldn't help but feel like there was some sort of mistake.

"You just spread your legs like a whore, not caring who you're hurting."

"I don't know who you are," I said, trying to keep my voice steady. "I've never met you before in my life. And I don't know who your boyfriend is… And I don't dress up like a girl!"

But the woman didn't believe me. She kept shouting and pointing, her anger growing with each passing moment. I could feel the eyes of the people around us, watching the scene with growing interest. I tried to walk away, but she followed me, screaming at me, making sure the audience of strangers grew exponentially by the minute.

Eventually, the woman stormed off, still shouting and gesturing. I was left standing on the street, feeling more confused and bewildered than ever.

People were staring at me, and I just stood there, pale-faced for a moment before shouting, "What do you all want?"

It was one of those moments that would have left me really, really wanting to smoke a cigarette… but now, those urges were gone. Instead of craving a smoke, I began to feel strangely lightheaded, like I needed to sit down.

It was a sensation that came over me often, since my hypnosis session. It almost seemed like that hypnotherapist had replaced my cravings for cigarettes with borderline flu-like symptoms. I almost felt feverish, now wanting to get home as quickly as possible. So that's what I did.

And as soon as I got home, I went to my bed to have a nap, even though it was only 2:00 PM. I'd never been a napper... not until I quit smoking. But they say that napping is a healthy thing to do.

I found myself in a strange dream, where I was no longer myself but a woman. I looked down at my body and was surprised to see that I had long hair and curves that were foreign to me. But before I could process what was happening, I noticed that every stranger I saw had a look of intense desire in their eyes.

Men and women alike were drawn to me, drawn to my feminine form. They approached me with open arms, trying to touch me or kiss me. I was taken aback by their aggressive behavior, but I couldn't help but feel a sense of excitement at the same time.

As I walked down the street, the strangers continued to approach me, trying to get closer and closer. Their faces were a blur, and their words were garbled, but their intent was clear - they wanted me.

I TRIED TO RUN, but they were everywhere, closing in on me from all sides. I could feel their breath on my skin, their hands reaching out to touch me. It was a feeling of both terror and exhilaration, and I didn't know how to escape.

Finally, I woke up, my heart racing and my body covered in sweat. I looked around the room, relieved to see that I was alone. It had all been a dream, but it had felt so real.

As I tried to make sense of what had happened, I couldn't help but feel disturbed by the dream.

Now, it was 10:00 PM. I napped for a full eight hours. My whole sleep schedule was destroyed. I had to work in about eight hours, but I knew that falling back asleep was impossible.

I went to my bathroom to have a shower. That's when I noticed some abnormalities. There were drips of water around my sink, as if someone had been splashing around in it. Some of that water was tinted black, as if it had ink in it. As I went to wipe up that water, I noticed something on my finger-nails: small flakes of white, as if I'd accidentally dipped my hands into paint, but failed to get all of the paint off before it dried on. It wasn't so easy to pick off either.

And then, as I showered, I noticed similar bits of white on my toenails, particularly near the cuticle. I worked hard to scrub it off, not wanting anyone to think that I'd been painting my nails... because I hadn't been painting my nails.

Emerging from the shower, I noticed another abnormality, something that just didn't add up: my ears were pierced. No, I wasn't wearing earrings, but there were little holes. I was sure that I'd never gotten my ears pierced before.

And the strangeness continued. I stepped out from the bathroom and suddenly smelled the strong scent of perfume: an undeniable female smell. I went around my apartment, smelling it everywhere. I assumed it was coming from one of the neigh-bours... but it was particularly strong in my bedroom, which was in the corner of the building.

I didn't like what was happening.

I tried to remain calm about it all, spending the night on my couch, watching TV because there was nothing else to do at that late hour. Honestly, the hours seemed to fly by quickly... unusually quickly.

At one moment, it was 2:00 AM... Then, it was suddenly 6:00 AM. And I could chalk it up to getting lost in the show that I'd been watching, but there was one detail that needed to be explained: I was in different clothes.

Yes, they were my own clothes, but they weren't the clothes that I was wearing... at least I didn't think that they were. To be honest, I never paid much attention to what I was putting on in the morning; I would just grab whatever was at the top of the pile. Now, I was wearing a green sweater and blue jeans, which wasn't a combo that I ever wore (they were colours that really didn't match).

But I brushed the anxiety away, assuming I was just experiencing a small blip.

I walked to work, lost in my thoughts, when I noticed something strange happening. Men kept glancing at me, as if they knew me, but I didn't recognize any of them.

At first, I thought it was all in my head, a figment of my imagination. But as I walked further, I noticed that it was happening more and more often. Men would turn their heads as I walked by, or they would stare at me from across the street.

I couldn't help but feel uneasy. I had never seen any of these men before, but it felt like they knew me. It was a strange and unsettling feeling, and I couldn't shake the sense of paranoia that was creeping in.

I tried to brush it off and keep walking, but the feeling of being watched was becoming more and more intense. I could feel eyes on me, even when I couldn't see the men who were watching.

Finally, I arrived at my workplace, feeling relieved to be off the street. But even there, I couldn't shake the sense of being watched. I felt like I was being scrutinized, like every move I made was being watched and analyzed.

It was a strange and disconcerting experience, and I couldn't help but wonder if it was all in my head. But as the day wore on, and I continued to feel the eyes of strangers on me, I began to wonder if there was something more to it. Maybe there was some sort of strange energy that was following me, or maybe there was a group of people who had it out for me.

Whatever the cause, I knew that I needed to be careful. The feeling of being watched was all-consuming, and I couldn't shake the sense of unease that it brought. I walked home, keeping my head down, trying to avoid the glances of strangers. It was a relief to be home, but I couldn't help but wonder when the feeling of being watched would return.

I just assumed that I was anxious and tired. And then, I showed up at my gym, to get a small workout in before I crashed for the night.

"I'm sorry," she said, holding her hand out, palm facing me, telling me to stop. "You need to go."

"Why?" I asked.

"Too many complaints. Honestly, you're lucky we don't call the cops for what you did. Not get out! Your membership is over here."

"What!?" I asked. "What are you even talking about right now? I didn't do anything!"

"I'm going to give you ten seconds to leave the premises, and then I'm calling the police."

"This is crazy!" I said. "I swear I didn't do anything! Can you at least tell me what it is I've been accused of doing?"

"It's too vulgar," she said, crossing her arms. "And the advances you made on our clients... It's unacceptable."

"Vulgar? What are you talking about?"

"Stealing clothes from the women's changing room… pushing yourself onto men who are trying to workout… bartering for sexual favours. People come here to workout. This isn't some filthy brothel!"

A large man came out from the back, arms bulging, scowl on his face. "Get out," he growled, and that was a man that I wasn't about to argue with; he had the strength to crush a skull with a single hand.

I stumbled out of that gym and hurried away from the building, not wanting to have my head kicked in. Three staff members stepped out to stare me down, warning me not to come back. "This is some sort of mistake!" I yelled. "I didn't do any of that stuff! You've got the wrong guy!"

I didn't even make it home before a stranger

called out to me, "Hey beautiful! Getting dolled up tonight?"

"Leave me alone!" I shouted.

I was living in a nightmare. I had no idea what the hell was happening to me. It almost was starting to seem like someone was playing a cruel prank on me. I was on the verge of tears, tense all over with intense anxiety.

It was one of those moments where I would have killed a man for a cigarette, back before I quit smoking. Now, I was getting that drowsy feeling: that lightheadedness that made it hard to walk in a straight line. I stumbled into my apartment, rushed over to the couch, and then I crashed with a dull thud, fall asleep instantly.

I found myself in another strange dream, where I

was getting dressed up like a girl. It was a feeling of excitement and anticipation, as I painted my nails and picked out the perfect outfit. I sorted through a drawer filled with panties: lacy panties, satin panties —and even whorish crotchless panties. I put my hand into the drawer to feel all of those fabrics, and then I moaned gleefully, my hair standing up on the back of my neck.

I looked like a princess with my blonde hair and bangs.

I had to pick out a dress: something cute, some-thing tight, something perfect…

I sorted through the options and then landed on the most perfectest of them all:

The dress was a vision of pink, with soft, delicate fabric that shimmered in the light. It was a piece of clothing that could make anyone feel like a princess, and I couldn't help but be drawn to it.

As I picked it up, I felt a sense of excitement coursing through my veins. It was the kind of dress that made you feel like you were living in a fairy tale, like anything was possible.

I slipped it on, feeling the fabric brush against my skin. It was soft and cool, clinging to my body in all the right places. I twirled around, feeling like a ballerina in a music box.

The dress fit me perfectly, hugging my curves and making me feel like the most beautiful woman in the world. Oh God! I loved that feeling so much! I moaned out with pleasure, as if the feeling of that fabric was enough to induce an orgasm. It was the kind of dress that made you stand up a little straighter, that made you feel like you could conquer anything.

As I looked at myself in the mirror, I couldn't help but smile. It was a feeling of pure joy, a moment of perfection that made all of the struggles of life fade away.

The pretty pink dress was more than just a piece of clothing - it was a symbol of hope and happiness, a reminder that sometimes, the smallest things can bring us the most joy.

I wanted to put on a different dress… something even more perfect than the pink dress.

I found a white dress: small and petite, with a short skirt. It went perfectly with the black heeled booties that I had my eye on.

I felt giddy with excitement as I put on the dress and twirled around my apartment. I was filled with a sense of joy and freedom, as if nothing could stop me from being myself.

I looked in the mirror and was amazed at how beautiful I looked. My hair was styled perfectly, my makeup was flawless, and my outfit was on point. I couldn't help but giggle with delight, feeling like the most beautiful woman in the world. "Princess Ophelia," I whispered in a girly voice. Then, I giggled.

As I skipped around my apartment, I felt a sense of lightness and freedom that I had never felt before.

It was like I had shed all of the baggage and expectations of my everyday life and was able to be completely myself.

The dream skipped ahead, as dreams do, and I was suddenly in a club, filled with people dancing, drinking, laughing. The music was loud and the lights were low. I swirled into the room, feeling amazing in my cute white dress. All eyes quickly turned to me. I could feel the men ogling me, devouring me with their eyes. I caught myself winking at them... and then worse: I would walk up to them and brush my fingers over their cocks. I would bite my lip and stare into their eyes, watching as they became hypnotized by me.

Then, I would giggle, thrilled that I had so much power.

I danced with men. I sang along to songs. I drank shot after shot after shot. I ran my fingers through my long blonde hair. Oh God, I was having so much fun.

Then, as dreams do, everything skipped ahead. I was in the bathroom with a man. He had his hands on me. He was kissing my body. Then, I went down to my knees. I grabbed his big, fat cock, and I began to pump it, aiming it at my face. "Come on me," I said to him. "Fuck my face and come on me."

He groaned and I squeezed harder.

"Fucking come on my face!" I screamed.

And then, I was suddenly awake, in my apartment, gasping for air. I rushed over to the mirror and was relieved to see that I was not a blonde woman; I was just myself.

I sat on the edge of my bed, feeling lost and confused. The strange dreams that had been haunting me for weeks wouldn't stop, and I couldn't help but wonder if I was losing my mind.

As I thought back on the dreams, I couldn't shake the sense of unease that they brought. They were so vivid and strange, and I couldn't help but wonder what they meant… and if they were related at all to the strange accusations from strangers.

I was still too afraid to go anywhere near that gym.

And then there were the looks on the street - the glances from strangers that seemed to follow me everywhere I went. At first, I had thought it was all in my head, but now I wasn't so sure. It was like there was something out there, watching me, and I couldn't escape it.

I felt a sense of panic rising in my chest. What if I was having a mental breakdown? What if I was losing touch with reality? It was a terrifying thought, and I didn't know what to do.

I tried to push the thoughts out of my mind and go about my day, but the sense of unease wouldn't go away. Every person who looked at me, every strange dream that I had, seemed to be a sign that something was wrong.

As the day wore on, I found myself growing more and more agitated. I couldn't focus on my work, and I felt like the world was closing in on me. It was a feeling of complete helplessness, and I didn't know how to escape it.

I knew that I needed help, but I didn't know who to turn to. It was a feeling of complete isolation, and I couldn't help but wonder if I was the only one who had ever felt this way.

As I lay down to sleep, I couldn't shake the sense of fear that was consuming me. It was like I was trapped in my own mind, unable to escape the strange dreams and the constant feeling of being watched.

Then, I remembered that hypnotherapy session. Now, it seemed like a long-distant memory: almost three months earlier. But I couldn't help but feel that woman had done this to me. When she went into my brain to fix my smoking addiction, she must have broken something. She must have crossed some wire with some other wire and created this whole catastrophe.

I remembered that she had a no-refund policy… but that didn't mean that she had a no-corrections policy. This was possibly all her fault, after all, and maybe she would be inclined to address the issue if it meant avoiding a lawsuit.

So I called the office. I waited on hold for forty minutes before I finally got to speak to the calm receptionist with the cult-like tone in her voice. "I really need to talk to the doc," I said.

"She can only speak to you if you have an appointment," she said.

"It's important. She messed me up and I need her to fix me, alright? It probably won't take more than ten minutes."

"I'm afraid I can't facilitate that," she said with an unnervingly calm smile in her voice. "Is there anything else I can help you with today?" For a moment, I wondered if I was talking to a robot.

"Please," I said. "Just listen to me. Weird things have been happening since I was in a few months ago. She did something to me. I—I don't know what, but I'm sure she knows. Please just go and get her."

"I'm sorry, sir. I can put you on the waitlist, but I should mention that you will have to pay for the appointment."

I took a deep breath and launched into my last

attempt at a plea. "I need to see Dr. Lee as soon as possible. It's an emergency. I'm having these strange dreams and I can't shake the feeling of being watched. Please, is there any way you can fit me in? There must be something you can do for me!"

The receptionist didn't sound convinced. "I'm sorry, sir, but Dr. Lee's schedule is completely booked for the next year. You'll have to go on the waitlist like everyone else." Her voice was finally starting to lose that cult-like fairness. She was getting annoyed with me. I wondered if the doctor told her about my outburst after my session.

I felt a sense of panic rising in my chest.

A year?

I couldn't wait that long. I needed help now. "Please, I'm begging you. Is there anything you can do?"

But the receptionist was firm. "I'm sorry, sir, but there's nothing I can do. We have a long waitlist, and Dr. Lee's schedule is completely full. You'll just have to wait your turn like everyone else."

I hung up the phone, feeling a sense of despair and hopelessness. How was I supposed to wait a year for help? The dreams and the feeling of being watched weren't going to go away on their own. And worse: all of those strange accusations. Did they have something to do with all of this?

No, it wasn't possible. Those accusations were just absurd! If they were even remotely true, that meant that I was blacking out and living some sort of second life as a woman. It was just impossible. I didn't have women's clothes. I didn't have makeup. I didn't have nail polish or women's shoes... and I didn't look anything like a woman!

I went to the closet to grab my laundry bin, to take it down to the basement of the building to run a load. There, I noticed a box. I opened it nervously. Then, I screamed (much like a girl, mind you) when I saw the disembodied head staring back at me. I fell back and scrambled away from the severed head before realizing that it was the head of a mannequin, wearing a long blonde wig...

"W—What the hell?" I said. Why was this in my apartment? Who put it there? Why was it hidden in a box?

My heart fell into the pit of my stomach.

I knew what this meant, and I knew that it was not good.

I stared at it in disbelief. I didn't remember buying it, and I couldn't imagine why I would ever need a wig like this. It was like a piece of someone else's life, something that didn't belong to me.

And then it hit me. What if I had worn the wig before, during one of my blacked-out episodes? What if there were parts of my life that I couldn't remember, things that I had done or said that were beyond my control?

The thought was terrifying. It was like a ghostly

suggestion that I was living in two worlds: one that I knew, and one that was hidden from me. It was a feeling of being lost and out of control, unable to remember what I had done or who I had been.

As I stared at the wig, I couldn't help but wonder what other secrets my life held. What other things had I done that I couldn't remember? It was a feeling of uncertainty and fear, and I didn't know how to escape it.

That damned doctor did this to me. I was going to sue her. I was going to end her career! How could she do this to a person!?

How could I prove it? How could I even afford a lawyer to try?

I put the wig back in the box, feeling like I was burying a piece of my past. I should have just thrown it away, but I was afraid to mess with it, as if it was some cursed, possessed thing that would be easily aggravated. I figured I could just leave it alone; maybe the police would need it as evidence one day…

Then came one of those anxious moments that would have normally been satisfied with a cigarette or two. A lightheadedness washed over me and I stumbled over to my bed before I fell down like someone suffering from intense narcolepsy. Within seconds, I was out cold... and then came the dreams —dreams that were now all too familiar—dreams that I wished would go away.

I suppose they were nightmares, even though I was perfectly content, satisfied, and happy while they'd played out.

I found myself in a strange dream, trapped in my own body as if I was possessed. I was at the mall, dressed up like a girl, and men were flirting with me, touching me, but I was unable to control what was happening.

It was like a nightmare, a feeling of being stuck in a body that wasn't mine, unable to stop what was happening around me. I could feel the touch of their hands on my skin, and it made me feel sick, like I was living in a world that wasn't my own.

It was so realistic. One man even cupped my ass and squeezed. I wanted to spin around and slap him, but I was possessed by an entity that liked being touched, fondled, groped. I turned around and grabbed him by the cock, massaging, squeezing. "Want to fuck me?" I asked the man.

He bit his lip and looked down my body. "I want to pound your pussy so fucking hard," he growled.

"I have a cock," I said. "But you can suck it if you want. Or you can just fuck my asshole. It's up to you."

I had no control over what I was saying. I was just stuck there, watching...

The man took me into the mall bathroom. He pushed me to my knees and forced me to suck his cock, and I had to suffer through every second. The dream just wouldn't end. It was so awful....

But at the same time, there was a strange sense of enjoyment that I couldn't explain. It was like I was living a double life, one where I was trapped in my own body, unable to control what was happening, and another where I was a different person entirely, able to flirt and tease without fear or shame.

I let the man ejaculate on my face while I roared with laughter. "Yes!" I screamed. "Cum on my fucking face! Cum on my fucking face!" I had no control over the volume of my voice. I felt every hot, gooey blast.

As the dream went on, I found myself growing more and more confused. It was like I was living in two worlds, unable to reconcile the person I was with the person I wanted to be.

I went straight back into that mall and got right back to eyeing strangers, grinning at them, inviting them over to talk to me. I let them touch me. I touched them.

And then the dream was over, leaving me feeling lost and uncertain.

Thank God it was over. I couldn't take anymore...

I went to my bathroom and stared at myself in the mirror, looking into my own eyes. Then, I noticed a slight black smear under my eyes. I tried to rub it away, but it was stuck there, stained. It took fifteen minutes to scrub it away.

What was it?

I sat alone in my apartment, staring out the window at the bustling city below. It was a feeling of unease that I couldn't shake, a sense of uncertainty and confusion that seemed to follow me wherever I went.

As I thought back on the strange dreams that had been haunting me, I couldn't help but wonder... were they real?

It was like I was living in two worlds - one that I knew, and one that was hidden from me.

But what if the dreams were real? What if they were actually happening? What if I was putting that wig on that was in the closet, and heading out in the world? It was a terrifying thought, and I didn't know how to make sense of it.

I tried to shake the feeling of uncertainty, to convince myself that the dreams were just that: dreams. But there was a part of me that couldn't let go, a part of me that was horrified of the possibility of something more.

No—it was impossible. Sure, there was a mysterious wig in my apartment… but a wig isn't enough to transform a person. It's not like I could just slap a blonde wig on my head and turn into a woman who could go into public and seduce men. In my last dream, the man was convinced that I was a real woman; he even mentioned my 'pussy'.

What if there was more than a wig in my apartment? What if the rest of that 'disguise' was hidden around?

I searched through my apartment, my heart racing with fear and uncertainty. I didn't know what I was looking for, but there was a sense of urgency that I couldn't shake. I knew that I could answer these horrible questions in my head if I could just confirm that there was nothing more than that strange wig.

As I rummaged through my front-hall closet, I stumbled upon a box that I didn't recognize. I opened it, and to my horror, I found it filled with dresses, skirts, blouses, and lingerie.

Lace, satin, latex. One outfit even had a crotch hole for 'easy access' during intercourse. "My God..." I whispered.

But that wasn't all. As I dug deeper, I found a container of makeup: lipstick, eyeliner, blush— everything that a woman might use to enhance her beauty—or what a man might use to disguise himself as a genuine woman.

My mind was racing. I didn't remember buying any of this, and I couldn't imagine why it would be in my apartment. It was like a piece of someone else's life, something that didn't belong to me.

"No, no, no," I whispered.

And then it hit me: what if I had worn the dresses before, or used the makeup? What if there were parts of my life that I couldn't remember, things that I had done or said that were beyond my control?

The thought was terrifying. If that stuff was real, then the dreams were possibly real. And if the dreams were real, then that meant that I'd been with men: I'd sucked off strangers. I'd allowed men to push their fat, erect cocks into my asshole. Men had ejaculated onto my face, into my mouth. I could even remember one horrible dream where I rubbed the warm cum all over my chest and crotch…

But it wasn't a dream.

I put the dresses and the makeup back in the box. My hands were trembling. I was short of breath. I felt like I was going to faint.

My apartment was a complete disaster. I had spent the last twenty minutes tearing through my things in a frantic search for something, anything that would give me a clue to what was happening to me.

I prayed that the existence of that girly attire was just some sort of coincidence… but how else could it be explained?

Clothes were strewn all over the floor, drawers were pulled out and emptied, and papers were scattered everywhere. It was like a storm had ripped through the place, leaving chaos and destruction in its wake.

As I looked around, the air was thick with dust and the smell of sweat. I could feel my heart racing with fear and desperation.

I was getting light-headed. I felt like I needed to lay down and close my eyes… but I didn't want it to happen again. I didn't want to live through another one of those dreams… which weren't dreams at all, but hours of my life that I had no control over, and very little memory of.

It was a scene of pure desperation and helplessness, a place where something terrible had happened and the aftermath was all that was left. As I tried to put things back in order, I felt that lightheadedness growing, begging me to move to my couch, to close my eyes for just a minute…

But I tried to fight it. I couldn't let it take me. I couldn't succumb to it again.

Suddenly, I blacked out, face-planting into the hard, cold floor.

CHAPTER 3

J stood before my mirror, blonde hair on my head. I was carefully putting lipstick on my lips, humming a cute little tune. My eyes were already done: eyeliner, mascara, and a soft blue eyeshadow that had a bit of a 90s vibe to it.

I was happy with how I was looking, but I wasn't quite finished. Next to me, a video was playing on my laptop: a makeup tutorial video.

"Hey everyone, it's Kiera, your favourite beauty influencer here, and today I'm going to be showing you how to create the perfect everyday makeup look.

"First things first, you want to start with a good base. Make sure you've got your moisturizer on and then apply your favourite primer. This will help your makeup last all day and prevent any creasing or fading.

"Next, it's time to apply your foundation. I like to use a beauty blender for this, but you can use whatever tool you prefer. Just make sure to blend it in really well, especially around your jawline and hairline.

"After that, it's time to cover up any blemishes or dark circles with concealer. I like to use a lighter shade to brighten up the under-eye area and then a shade that matches my skin tone to cover any blemishes.

"Now it's time for the fun part - adding some colour to your face! I like to use a peachy blush on the apples of my cheeks and then add some high-lighter to the tops of my cheekbones, the bridge of my nose, and my cupid's bow. Here's a little trick: blush on the top of your nose. I know it seems weird, but stick with me. It's, like, the cutest little detail ever. See? Isn't that so adorable?

"Lastly, it's time to add some colour to your lips. I like to use a neutral pink shade for an everyday look, but you can use whatever colour you like best.

"And there you have it - the perfect everyday makeup look. Just remember to have fun with it and make it your own! Thanks for watching, and I'll see you in the next one." She blew a kiss at the screen and then, for some strange reason, I blew a kiss back.

Now that I knew this wasn't just a 'dream', I felt more present. I was more aware of what was happening. I wasn't drifting in and out quite as much. I was conscious, but still entirely out of control. I was still stuck watching every minute, helpless. I almost wished that I could go back to the way it was, where the whole 'dream' was nothing but a blur, with a few strange memories here and there.

I didn't want to know what I was going to end up doing.

I looked at myself in the mirror, still not quite

believing what I was seeing. I had spent hours getting ready - doing my makeup, putting on my blonde wig, and picking out the perfect dress.

The blonde wig had long, straight hair with delicate, wispy bangs that framed my face. It was made from soft, silky fibres that felt surprisingly natural against my skin. When I put it on, it transformed me into someone else entirely, someone who was more confident, more beautiful, more alive.

And now, looking at my reflection, I realized that I really did pass as a woman. My makeup was flawless, my hair was perfect, and my dress was cute and stylish… though short and skimpy.

It was a moment of both excitement and fear, a realization that I could be anyone I wanted to be, that I could live a different life if I chose to.

But even as I grappled with these conflicting emotions, I couldn't help but feel a sense of confidence—confidence that I absolutely was not used to having… confidence that didn't belong.

I had this alien thought in my head: feeling like anything was possible, and I was finally free to be whoever I wanted to be. But that's not who I wanted to be! I wanted to be myself, not some blonde slut.

And I really was dressed like a slut. That dress was tiny, with a skirt so short that my ass was out to anyone who wanted to see it.

But my God! The frilly white shoulders of the dress felt so amazing against my skin. The sheer fabric was so light and airy. I felt so free, even though my whole body was on display. But whatever was in control of my body simply didn't care that I was totally exposed.

Before leaving the apartment, I watched myself head into the kitchen. I dug into the far end of my medicine cabinet, producing a small orange pill bottle. I took three of those little pills. What was I taking?

Then, I went back to the mirror, looking at my chest through that sheer fabric. I watched myself as I cupped my own chest, squeezing my non-existent tits. What the hell was I doing? Why was I now massaging my pecs?

I tried hard to wake myself up from that dream… No—it wasn't a dream. It was a hypnotized state. I knew that I could take control of my body again—I just didn't know how to do it. I tried straining. I tried focussing as hard as I could, trying to over-power the poltergeist that was in control.

And for a brief moment, I managed to make myself stop. I managed to override that hypnotic programming. I forced myself to look down at my hands, seeing that I'd painted my nails a soft white. "No," I managed to say, as if I was trying to talk some sense into myself. "You aren't doing this."

But the feminine pushed back. The girl inside of me was determined to go out and have her fun, using me against my will. After a few seconds, I was on the street, humming that cute little tune under my breath. And within a minute, I was smiling at strangers, winking at me, and even twirling around as the soft breeze tickled my skin.

People stopped to look at me, probably thinking that I was high on ecstasy. I just giggled, not caring what they thought. But where was I going?

I stopped at a street corner of a busy intersection. A man stepped up next to me, clutching a briefcase. I looked at him, staring right into his eyes. I tried hard to force myself to look away, but that female demon that was in control was too powerful.

Finally, the man looked over and returned the smile. "Good morning," he said.

"That suit looks super hot on you," I said.

He blushed, tensing up all over. Then, he laughed nervously. "Um, thanks. I, uh, like your dress too. It really suits your figure."

"You can fuck me in it, if you want," I said.

His eyes grew wide. The light turned green and he scuttled away, tense, nervous, probably thinking that I was a prostitute. And honestly, I was starting to wonder if I was a prostitute. Maybe that's what I'd been doing during those black-outs: selling myself to any man who wanted me. After all, I afforded that wig and those clothes somehow.

The feminine inside of me spotted a hefty man across the road. I crossed when it was clear, and approached him directly. "Hey, big boy," I smiled. He turned to look at me, looking me up and down, seeing through my sheer dress.

"Can I help you?" he asked.

"I'm working," he said. He was organizing a fruit stand outside of a busy grocery store.

"When do you go on break?"

"Why?" he asked, narrowing his gaze.

"I bet you have a big, fat cock," I said. "I'd love to suck you off."

He turned white, freezing. He stuttered, and then

he looked around. "I, uh, need to head inside." He rejected me, scurrying off.

And now I knew why so many people recognized me, and why I'd been banished from so many shops and venues.

Next, I arrived at a rundown gas station. It was a sad and sorry sight, like a relic from a bygone era. The pumps were old and rusted, with peeling paint and faded signs. The building itself was made of weathered wood, with a sagging roof and broken windows. There was a flickering neon sign that read "open", but it was clear that the place had seen better days. The lot was empty, with only a few scattered pieces of trash blowing in the wind. It was a place that was forgotten and ignored. I went through the door, and then the cashier sprung to his feet. "No," he said. "You get out! Out!" He had a thick Middle-Eastern accent. "Get out or I'm calling the cops."

My heart fluttered down into the pit of my stomach. I didn't know what I'd done, but I had some terrible ideas.

I just grinned at him. "If you let me stay, I'll make it worth if for you," I said.

"This isn't a brothel!" he shouted. "You carved that hole into that bathroom wall! Do you know how much it cost me to patch that hole!?"

Oh God—what had I done? Was he telling me that I'd made a glory-hole in his gas station bathroom?

I couldn't help but wonder just how many times I'd been out as a girl. Had this been going on since the day of the hypnosis? That was months ago now... Just how many men had I been with in that time?

I ran off, being chased away by the gas station owner. And a normal, sane person would have gone straight home to hide away in shame, but the whore inside of me wasn't satisfied—or even fazed by the humiliation. She just went on to the next place: a downtown mall that was busy with businessmen, now getting off for lunch.

The downtown mall was a bustling hub of activity, filled with businessmen and women who were out on their lunch break. The air was thick with the smell of food, coffee, and the hustle and bustle of people going about their day. For a moment, I felt invisible, almost relieved to be in a big crowd where everyone had their own lives and their own problems.

Amidst the crowds, there was a small barbershop, where men in sharp suits were getting their hair trimmed and styled. The barbers were skilled, their scissors and clippers moving with precision as they transformed their clients' hair into perfectly groomed styles.

Outside the barbershop, the mall was a flurry of activity. People hurried past, clutching bags of shopping, talking on their phones, and rushing to make their appointments. The sound of footsteps echoed off the polished tile floors, and the hum of conversation filled the air.

There were restaurants and cafes, with the smells of fresh food wafting out into the corridors. The bright lights of the mall illuminated the faces of the people who hurried by, each with their own purpose and destination.

I stood in the middle of that busy place, near a large water feature, which occasionally misted me with a pleasant moisture. I looked around slowly, scanning. And it was a moment before I realized exactly what I was doing: looking for a target.

I was like the Predator, or the Terminator, scanning all of the potential victims in that area, trying to pick out one that was bound to cave to me. I stood in the middle of the bustling mall, my heart racing as I scanned the crowds of people, looking for the perfect 'victim'. Dressed as a girl, with my blonde wig and cute dress, I felt more confident and alive than I ever had before.

As I looked around, I searched for someone who looked like an easy target, someone who might be flattered by my attention and willing to indulge my growing addiction to male attention. It was a dangerous game, but one that I couldn't resist.

And then I saw him: a man in a sharp suit, his eyes scanning the shops and stores around him. He looked confident and successful, and I knew that he would be the perfect person to approach. There was just something about him: a cockiness that showed on the grin on his face. I watched him as a pretty young woman passed him, and he turned around to stare at her bum, even licking his lips as his eyes bulged slightly from his head.

He almost seemed too easy.

But in that moment, I wanted someone easy, someone who wasn't going to reject me, because my hunger for cock was growing. I was practically squirming, trying to resist the urge to simply throw myself at a random man, to rip down his pants, to plunge his cock into my mouth. I knew doing something stupid like that would get me arrested, but if I couldn't find a man to take me soon, there was a good chance that I would end up in the back of a police cruiser, being added to some sex offender list.

As I made my way over to the sharp man, my heart pounding with excitement and fear, I could feel the eyes of the people around me on me. But I didn't care. All that mattered was the rush of adrenaline that came with the pursuit.

And as I approached him, my mind already racing with thoughts of what might happen next, I felt a sense of freedom and power that I had never known before. Finally, his gaze looked up, meeting mine. He paused for a moment as I grinned.

The sun beamed down through one of the skylights, seeming to cast a golden spotlight right on him, like the universe was handing him to me as a sort of divine gift.

I stopped in front of him and let him scan my body. I bit my lip and said, "Lunch break?"

"Want to get lunch with me?" he asked.

He was tall and lean, with chiseled features and a confident stride. His hair was dark and styled perfectly, and he wore a sharp suit that fit him like a glove.

I caught a whiff of his cologne: a musky, masculine scent that was both alluring and powerful. It made my heart race even faster, and I felt a surge of desire that I couldn't ignore.

Our eyes met, and for a moment, I felt like I was under a spell. There was something magnetic and intoxicating about him, something that made me want to surrender to my every desire.

It was a dangerous game, but one that I couldn't resist in that hypnotized state. I took a deep breath and stepped closer, feeling the heat of his body as we stood face to face. And even as I felt the thrill of the chase, I knew that I was playing with fire, and that there would be consequences to my actions. "Fuck lunch," I said. "I just want you to bend me over and fuck me."

His eyes beamed. He stuttered for a moment before letting out a nervous laugh. He looked around, trying to decide if he was being pranked, and then he looked back at me. "You serious?"

I nodded my head.

He didn't need much convincing. He grinned, and then he said, "Lead the way, beautiful."

I led him through the mall. It wasn't a mall that I'd ever been in before... at least that's what I thought. I knew the way through it. I knew to go upstairs, and then I found the hallway that went down to the service closets and storage rooms. I took the man down a long back corridor, and then we found the storage room of a shoe store, filled with shoe boxes.

The room was cramped and cluttered, with rows of dusty cardboard boxes stacked haphazardly against the walls.

The only source of light was a single flickering bulb that cast eerie shadows on the walls, making it difficult to see what was stored in the boxes. The air was musty and thick, with the smell of old leather and dust.

The room was filled with the sounds of scurrying rats and the distant hum of the mall's HVAC system. The only thing that broke the silence was the occasional creaking of the floorboards as we made my way through the maze of boxes.

Within moments of being in that room, I was undressing. I took off that tiny white dress and then turned to the man, naked.

"Oh shit," he said, looking down. "You're trans."

I nodded my head with a smile. "You don't have to touch it if you don't want," I said softly in that feminine voice. "Or, if you want, you can suck it and play with it. It's up to you."

He hesitated for a moment before coming up to me. He put his hands on me, caressed my skin and then he leaned in, kissing me on the neck. His musky cologne filled my nostrils. I let out a soft moan. His lips moved down my body. He found my nipples and began to suck.

I cannot begin to describe the intensity that came next; my nipples were insanely sensitive, making me tingle all over. He sucked hard, making them swell, becoming erect. I reached down and gripped his shaft through his black slacks. I grabbed hard and pumped, feeling the blood rushing into his member.

And again, I tried hard to regain control of myself, of my life. I tried to right the ship that was my body, but the feminine ghost that was commanding me would not relinquish control. I tried so hard, but it was a pointless fight, leaving me feeling mentally exhausted as I was forced to watch like a prisoner in my own body.

I watched as I dropped to my knees, as I fished out his erection, as I sucked his cock. I watched as he began to face-fuck me, thrusting in and out of my throat, grunting and groaning. I felt everything: every warm, throbbing vein. I felt his bulging tip. I felt him grabbing my hair and pulling. Luckily, I had about ten bobby pins holding my wig on, but that just made it hurt when he pulled.

I moaned.

"I fucking love it when you fuck my face," I said, looking up at him, with saliva all over my lips and chin.

He pushed his veiny cock back into my mouth and used me like a fuck-toy for another few minutes.

Next, I was on my hands and knees. He mounted me from behind. He penetrated me with his finger, pushing far into my asshole. Then, he stuck in a second finger. I moaned in pleasure as a terrible dread consumed me.

I was about to be fucked by a man, and I had no control over it.

He stepped in close, sliding his saliva-slicked cock between my ass cheeks. He groaned a loud groan, and then he spat, adding a bit more saliva to make it a bit more slippery. I felt his gob of spit trickling down my ass crack.

I felt his hands gripping my hips. I felt his tip finding my hole. Then, I closed my eyes as he pushed into me, filling my tight asshole with a fat, throbbing cock.

He pumped me, relentlessly. He was a man with no regard for his partner, me. I screamed out loud, feeling my insides being stretched mercilessly. It would have been nice to be eased into it, but the whore controlling my body was perfectly fine with what she was getting.

"You're so fucking tight," he growled, gripping me hard with both hands. He plunged fiercely down into my body. I felt his huge cock ripping into my insides.

It hurt, but there was an intense feeling of satisfaction. I stopped trying to fight. I let him own me. I went limp and gave in to the dominating presence of the powerful man. It was strangely freeing, letting go, even if it was just for a few minutes... He only lasted a few minutes.

But those few minutes were enough to satisfy all of the intense, powerful urges that had driven me to putting on that wig, that makeup, that little dress. It was all worth it. In that moment, I felt the exact same that I felt after a long, stressful day, when I would light up a cigarette and allow the smoke to fill my lungs.

In that moment, I knew that the hypnotherapist

traded in my smoking addiction for a new addiction: one that was much more dangerous and certainly much more shameful. She took away my desire for cigarettes and replaced it with a desire to be owned and dominated by men.

Satisfied, with an ass full of a stranger's cum, I made my way home. I walked in the door of my apartment, showered, retrieved some nail polish to remove the white from my fingernails, stashed away the wig and the dress, and then I sat on the toilet and pushed the cum out of my body. A minute later, I went to the floor where I blacked out, settled down, closed my eyes, and then I opened them again.

And then, it was just as if I hadn't gone out as a woman. It was as if the whole thing was like a dream... but now, I knew that it wasn't.

CHAPTER 4

I couldn't keep living like that. A week went by, and in that week, I must have blanked out ten times, losing easily twenty to thirty hours of my life. Sometimes I would be present and conscious (but out of control), and sometimes I would just be completely oblivious to what was happening, and I would wake up confused and frightened.

One particular instance put me over the edge, making me realize I needed to address this issue before it went any further. I woke up in my bed, in the middle of the day, with a sore ass, and there was a puddle of cum on my mattress that suggested four men had ejaculated inside of me. The soreness suggested the same; and maybe they tried to be inside of me at the same time.

I was lucky that I wasn't infested with STDs! I was lucky that I hadn't come across some angry person who figured I was better off dead.

Now, I couldn't go out in public; it seemed like I was recognized everywhere I went. The moment I stepped outside of my apartment, people would look at me. I started running all of my errands on the other end of town, but even there, gazes would turn to me and eye me questionably. And the strangers continued approaching me. "If you want to get dolled up tonight, I'll make it worth your while," said one stranger into my ear, as I stood and waited for the train.

Another stranger told me that I gave him the best blowjob of his life. "Whenever I masturbate, I think about that blowjob," he said with a smirk.

I was reduced to tears, rushing into a bathroom and locking myself in a stall. It was horrible, having absolutely no control over my life, knowing that I could slip into that state of unconsciousness at any moment.

It seemed to happen whenever I was stressed out about something: whenever I would normally turn to cigarettes.

I tried throwing out the wig, the clothes, and the makeup—but somehow, I would get my hands on new stuff. I would see the charges on my credit card: purchases at the mall, at wig shops, at makeup stores, and so on. And each time, the haul would be hidden somewhere else in my house, as if my feminine identity was trying to keep it hidden from my male identity.

I eventually stopped throwing it out, realizing I would go broke if that alternate persona kept spending money to replace it.

A truly frightening moment came when I got out of the shower one evening and saw, in the mirror, that I had lumps on my chest: the forming of breast tissue, pushing out, giving me something between an A-cup and a B-cup. I felt sick—so sick that I puked in the toilet. My nipples had doubled in size. I looked like I had the body of a teen girl, and there was a soreness in my chest, as if those 'breasts' were still growing.

Then, I remembered the pills. I rushed to the medicine cabinet and rifled through it until I found the strange orange bottle. I searched the name online and found that they were estrogen pills.

How long had I been taking them? Where did I get them?

I threw them in the trash, but the next day, they were back: a new bottle. While I thought I was sleeping, my second persona must have gone out to retrieve a new bottle. A week later, my breasts were noticeably bigger. My testicles were noticeable smaller. I was losing muscle mass, gaining fat on my hips and in my thighs. I was transforming into a woman, against my own will.

One afternoon, I woke up to the smell of toxic bleach. I scanned my whole apartment for the source of the smell, then, in the mirror, I saw that the smell was coming from my head. Now, I was blonde. My shaggy hair was now more sand-toned, matching that wig. In a panic, I rushed to grab my electric razor. I plugged it in, turned it on, and then something stopped me, like an invisible hand gripping my wrist, not allowing me to shave my head.

I tried hard to fight myself. I was determined to sabotage the female apparition that was taking over my body—but she was stronger than me. She fought me until I was exhausted… And then came one of those terrible moments of lightheadedness. I went to lay down, and then I blacked out, off to be a whore against my will.

I remember flashes of that particularly blackout. I remember being with a man and a woman, possibly a couple. We were in the back room of a club, all naked. My cock was in the mouth of the woman, and the man's cock was in my mouth. I sucked him until he came on my tongue, and then the woman forced me onto my hands and knees while the man held me in place. She pushed her fist into my asshole and plunged. She told me that she wasn't going to stop until I was ejaculating—and she succeeded in making it happen after fifteen sore, brutal, intense minutes.

And I knew it wasn't a dream because I couldn't walk for a day; the pain was too intense in my ass.

I spent that painful day trying to phone Dr. Sandra Lee, the hypnotherapist who cursed me with this horrible condition. I only got her receptionist, who kept telling me I had to wait on the waiting list, which I was already on. "You don't understand," I said. "This is an emergency."

But she didn't care.

I decided to go into the office, to try to force my way in to see Dr. Lee, which turned out to be a mistake. The receptionist told me to leave after telling me Dr. Lee was busy. "But it's an emergency," I said.

"I know that," she said with a groan. "That's what you said on the phone. But it's not really an emergency. You aren't dying. It's as much an emergency for you as it is for anyone else, and everyone else is on the waiting list. Now please leave."

I fought with her. I argued and then I started yelling. She told me that she was going to call security. "Fine! I dare you to call security! Do it!" I shouted.

And then she did it. Worse, she took my name off of the waitlist and told me that I wasn't welcome to return. "You can't do this to me!" I shouted.

But before I was pulled away, I caught a glimpse of the schedule on her desk. I saw the list of names. I saw that she had a 3:30 PM appointment in a day with a woman named Iva Claire. I even saw Iva's phone number and address as the security guard's arms wrapped around me. I took mental note of that address, and then I was pulled away.

Now, I had a plan: a desperate plan, but I was desperate. I got into my crappy little car and started up the clunking engine. I drove across town, my hands sweating on the steering wheel as I tried to steady my nerves. I knew that what I was about to do was crazy, even dangerous, but I was desperate. I needed to borrow her identity, her life, and if this failed, I had no other options. If I couldn't get back into Dr. Lee's office, then I would suffer from this debilitating illness for the rest of my life.

As I drove, my mind raced with thoughts of what might happen. What if I got caught? What if the woman recognized me, like so many other people? What if she called the police? What if I was making a huge mistake?

But even as I felt the weight of my fears bearing down on me, I couldn't stop myself. I was driven by a sense of desperation and a need for change, to rid myself of this feminized curse, and I knew that there was no turning back.

When I finally arrived at the woman's house, I parked my car down the street and tried to steady my breathing. I knew that I had to be careful, that I had to move quickly and decisively if I was going to get what I needed.

As I made my way up to the door, my heart pounding in my chest, I felt a sense of fear and antic-ipation that I had never felt before. I was stepping into the unknown, risking everything for a chance to fix my fucked-up life.

And even as I felt my mind starting to unravel, even as I began to lose my grip on reality, I knew that I had to keep moving forward. There was no turning back now, no second chances. This was it, the moment of truth.

The rough, poor residential part of town was a stark contrast to the glitz and glamour of the city's more affluent areas. The streets were littered with trash and debris, and the buildings were old and run-down, with cracked sidewalks and peeling paint.

The houses were small and cramped, with old cars and broken-down bicycles littering the yards. The air was thick with the smell of exhaust and pollution, and the sounds of barking dogs and shouting children echoed through the streets.

There was a sense of hopelessness and despair that hung over the neighbourhood, a feeling that life here was a struggle, a battle that was fought every day just to survive. And even though there were signs of life and vitality in the occasional community garden or children's playground, the overall feeling was one of sadness and neglect.

She answered the door after the second knock. She only opened the door a crack, careful not to allow me access to her home. "Can I help you?" she asked softly.

I was instantly taken aback by her stunning freckles. I had freckles like her when I was young, but they'd faded over time. Iva's were bold and beautiful, and they made her seem so stunningly innocent, filling me with a terrible guilt for what I was about to do to her.

Iva was a beautiful young woman, with long dark hair and bright, almond-shaped eyes. She had a delicate face, with high cheekbones and full lips that gave her an air of sophistication and elegance. But despite her beauty, she looked worn down by life's hardships. Her hair was unkempt, and her clothes were threadbare and old, with patches and tears here and there.

Iva's home was rundown and in disrepair, with peeling paint and a sagging roof. The windows were old and foggy, with cracks that let in the cold winter air. Inside, the home was small and cramped, with mismatched furniture and an air of neglect.

"Well?" she said.

"Iva Claire?" I said, trying to muster up a smile. It's hard to say exactly how Iva could afford a hypnotherapy session with Dr. Sandra Lee, one of the most expensive therapists in the province, given her apparent poverty and rundown living situation. However, there are a few possibilities.

One possibility is that Iva was able to obtain the funds for the therapy through a charitable organization or government program. It's possible that she was referred to Dr. Lee by a social worker or other professional, who recognized the need for her to receive the therapy and helped her obtain the necessary funds to pay for it.

Another possibility is that Iva may have sacrificed other basic needs or necessities to be able to pay for the therapy. For example, she may have foregone buying food or other essentials in order to save up for the session with Dr. Lee. This would be a risky and potentially dangerous decision, but it's possible that Iva felt that the therapy was worth the sacrifice.

It's also possible that Iva may have received financial assistance from a friend or family member who recognized the importance of the therapy for her well-being. This would be a more fortunate scenario, but it's certainly possible that Iva was able to find someone who was willing to help her pay for the expensive therapy.

As I peered into her home, I noticed a black lacy piece of lingerie resting on the back of a sofa chair, and the sight of the outfit made my heart race. I suddenly couldn't help but wonder if she'd whored herself out to make that money. Maybe she'd reduced herself to being a prostitute, just to gather the funds to see Dr. Lee, to rid herself of whatever was bothering her.

Given Iva's poverty and rundown living situation, there could have been a number of issues that she might have wanted to address with hypnotherapy from Dr. Lee.

One possibility was that Iva was dealing with stress and anxiety related to her financial struggles. She may have felt overwhelmed by her circumstances and the constant pressure to make ends meet, which could have been affecting her mental health and well-being. Hypnotherapy could have helped her to manage her stress and anxiety, allowing her to feel more calm and centred even in the face of difficult circumstances.

Another possibility was that Iva may have been dealing with trauma or other emotional issues related to her past experiences. If she had experienced abuse, neglect, or other traumatic events, this could have been affecting her current mental health and well-being. Hypnotherapy could have helped her to process these experiences and move forward in a more positive and healthy way.

Finally, it was possible that Iva may have been struggling with a specific issue or habit that she wanted to change. For example, she may have been struggling with an addiction or unhealthy behaviour that was holding her back from reaching her full potential. Hypnotherapy could have helped her to overcome this issue, giving her the tools and techniques she needed to make positive changes in her life.

Ultimately, there were many potential reasons why Iva might have sought out hypnotherapy with Dr. Lee, and it was difficult to say for sure what her specific goals might have been. Regardless of the reason, I was about to take the opportunity away from her, at least for a period of time. Sure, she could have rescheduled. She could get back onto that waitlist, and maybe they would even bump her up to the top of the list once they realized what I'd done... I tried not to think of who I was hurting to get what I needed. My own situation was increasingly desperate. It was only a matter of time before I ended up dead: beaten to death by some stranger who was less than excited to be hit on by some trans whore.

"Do you need something?" she asked.

"I'm with Dr. Sandra Lee's office," I said, producing a warm smile. "We tried to reach you over the phone, but we may have the wrong number in our system."

"I just got a call an hour ago from your office," she said, narrowing her eyes. "Confirming my appointment for tomorrow."

"Right, well, I've actually come here to tell you that Dr. Lee is unwell and will have to reschedule. Like I said: I tried calling, but the number in our system was for some downtown laundromat."

She had a confused look on her face. "She's sick?"

"Yes," I said. "About an hour ago, in fact—she started coughing and felt lightheaded. I'm sure it's just a flu, but she's going to take a few days off to rest. Then, we'll call you about rescheduling."

As I stared at her, I took note of all her features. I examined her long brown hair, her dark freckles, her blushing cheeks. I was going to need to recreate her look.

"Should I call the office now to reschedule?" she asked softly.

"No! No, no, no, don't do that. The office is closed for the day. You can call on, uh, Tuesday. That will be the best time to call. I'm really sorry about this, but we'll make sure to get you in right away to see Dr. Lee."

"O—Okay," she said.

I smiled, nodded my head, and backed away slowly. The guilt inside of me was strong.

Next, I stopped at a thrift store, to find an outfit.

I stepped into the shop, and was immediately struck by the musty smell of old clothes. The place was dimly lit, with flickering fluorescent lights overhead that gave everything a sickly, yellow hue. The aisles were narrow, and there were racks of clothes crammed together, leaving barely enough room to move. It was the perfect place to buy an outfit that some poor girl would have worn.

The clothes themselves were old and tattered, with faded colours and frayed edges. Most of them looked like they had been worn for years and then discarded, their owners moving on to something newer and better. There were rows of threadbare t-shirts, faded jeans with holes in the knees, and worn-out sneakers with scuffed soles.

Despite the shabby appearance of the clothing, there was a certain charm to the thrift store. There was a feeling of discovery in finding something that was one-of-a-kind, something that had a history and a story behind it. I could picture the person who had worn each item, wondering what their life was like and why they had given it up.

As I made my way through the store, I sorted through the clothes, pulling out a few girly items that caught my eye. But as I looked more closely, I began to see the flaws and imperfections - a stain on a shirt, a tear in a pair of pants, a missing button on a jacket. It was clear that these clothes were past their prime, and I was left wondering who would want to wear them.

I felt a wave of strange sensations washing over me. As my fingers grazed a satin dress, I paused. I looked at the dress and then my body tingled all over. It was a surprisingly cute little dress for that particular store: short, ruffled, with lace sleeves and a low-cut top. I picked it up and felt my body tingling all over with excitement. I wanted to wear that dress...

It was almost like that feminine demon was trying to force herself out of me, trying to take control even though it wasn't her turn. I didn't want to put that dress down. I wanted to feel it against my skin, all around me.

I wasn't there for cute dresses. I needed a tattered outfit that would make me look like Iva.

I forced myself away from the cute outfits and found some more appropriate attire. I found a sweater that was gently worn. Then, I found the perfect pair of jeans:

The tight jeans were made of a soft, stretchy fabric that had been worn just enough to fit the curves of the body perfectly. They were a deep, dark blue, with just a hint of fading at the seams and knees that suggested they had been gently worn over time. They hugged the body in all the right places, accentuating curves and creating a flattering silhouette. The waistline sat just above the hips, drawing attention to the narrowest part of the waist and creating a feminine shape. The fabric was soft and pliable, with just enough give to allow for easy movement.

As I looked more closely, I could see the fine details that made the jeans so special. The stitching was tight and precise, creating a clean and polished look. The back pockets were placed just right, drawing attention to the curves of the buttocks and creating a flattering look from every angle.

Despite being tight, the jeans were still comfortable to wear. The soft fabric felt good against the skin, and the waistband was snug without being constricting. The slight stretch in the fabric meant that the jeans moved with the body, creating a sense of ease and fluidity in movement.

I'd never looked at clothes like that before. Now, I felt almost hypnotized, analyzing the tiniest details of the clothing in that store. And it really did seem like I was hypnotized. Hardly realizing it, I spent two hours in that shop, sifting through nearly every single rack, feeling so many different fabrics against my skin.

And in that moment, a strange realization came to me: the feeling of the feminine attire was satisfying in the same way as a cigarette. While I was allowing myself to indulge in feeling clothes and trying on dresses (yes, I tried about six different dresses on), those lightheaded sensations stayed away. It was almost like I was getting my fix without having to blackout and allow that demon-whore to take me over.

To test my new theory, I bought more than just the tattered disguise that I would wear to Dr. Lee's office. I also bought a few cute dresses, a skirt, and some panties. I brought everything hole and put it on my bed. I satisfied those urges again by putting the clothes on my body, letting out a sigh of relief, as if I was taking a long drag from a smoke after a long, tedious day.

I fished some lingerie out from my closet. I put it on and sat in it while I watched television. For the first evening in months, I didn't have one of those strange episodes. I didn't slip into that feminine state of mind.

Maybe I was onto something. Maybe there was hope for me if Dr. Lee couldn't help me out.

Maybe I could control that other side of me more than I realized.

It was the next morning when I started to feel that lightheadedness coming on, right after I got off the phone with my now-ex-boss (he told me that I was no longer needed at work). I felt compelled to run to my bed, to rest, but I fought that urge and instead ran to the closet and pulled out my bag of feminine clothes.

As I dug through the bag filled with dresses and skirts, I couldn't help but feel excited by the possibilities. There was a delicate, floral-print sundress with a full skirt that swished as I moved, and a classic wrap dress in a rich, jewel-toned blue that would be perfect for a night out.

There were also several skirts to choose from, each with its own unique style. One was a flirty mini-skirt with a ruffled hem and a bold, graphic print, while another was a more demure midi-skirt in a soft, pastel hue. There was even a maxi-skirt with a daring high slit, perfect for making a statement at a summer party.

Oh God, the fabrics felt so fucking good against my skin.

In addition to the dresses and skirts, there were a few tops and blouses to mix and match. One was a sheer, lacy blouse that would look great with a pencil skirt, while another was a crisp white button-up that would be perfect for the office.

Each of the outfits was cute and stylish in its own way, and I couldn't wait to try them on and see how they looked. As I pulled each one out of the bag, I imagined all the different occasions where I could wear them - a casual brunch with friends, a romantic date, or even a fancy gala.

It was a few minutes before I realized the urge to pass out had gone away. I'd successfully fought it back, keeping control over my body. But to keep it away, I knew that I had to indulge, just a little bit. So I put on a black dress. I put on black heels. I put that wig on my head, and then I put on a touch of makeup. My God, it really was like smoking a cigarette... or five.

I relaxed into my couch, perfectly aware, perfectly conscious, perfectly in control.

And then I eyed the clock and saw that it was nearly time to go to my appointment, which was actually Iva's appointment.

I hated to get out of that dress, but I knew that I needed to dress the part. I put on the used sweater and and the worn jeans. At least the clothes were comfortable—and tight. I'd come to love the feeling of tight clothes against my skin; there was just something so, so satisfying about it.

I put on the girly sneakers I picked up at that same thrift store. Then, I found the brunette wig I picked up on the way home. I completed the outfit with the sheepskin jacket (also from the thrift store). And then came the makeup.

I looked through my search history and found which YouTube channel my alter ego used for makeup tutorials. I found the perfect tutorial to create a fake-freckle look.

"Hey everyone, it's your girl here, back with another makeup tutorial! Today, we're going to be creating a super trendy look with fake freckles. If you've ever wished you had a cute smattering of freckles on your face, but don't actually have them naturally, this tutorial is for you.

"To start, I'm going to use a lightweight foundation and apply it evenly all over my face. This will create a smooth, flawless base that will help the freckles look more natural.

"Now, we're going to create the freckles using a technique called "dotting." I'm going to use a brow pencil in a warm, golden brown shade, which will create a natural-looking freckle colour.

"Taking the pencil, I'm going to start by dotting it lightly across the bridge of my nose, and then gradually work outwards towards my cheeks and forehead. I'm making sure to vary the size and placement of the dots, so that they look as natural as possible.

"Once I'm happy with the placement of the freckles, I'm going to use a small brush to blend them in slightly. This will help to soften the edges and make them look more like natural freckles.

"Next, I'm going to add a bit of dimension to the freckles by using a slightly darker shade of brown. Using the same dotting technique as before, I'm going to add a few larger dots on top of the smaller ones, focusing on areas where the sun would naturally hit the face.

"Finally, I'm going to finish off the look with a light dusting of bronzer and a bit of mascara. The bronzer will help to give the face a sun-kissed glow, while the mascara will add definition to the eyes.

"And there you have it! A trendy, freckled look that's perfect for summertime. Give it a try and let me know how it turns out!"

I followed the tutorial to a tee, and the results were impressive. I couldn't help but wonder if Iva had learned to do her own makeup by following that exact same tutorial, because I really did look like her. I spent a few minutes practising my voice. I'm not sure how I was able to speak so convincingly like a girl when I was in that hypnotized state, but with some practise, I was able to get something decent— something that I was hopeful that Dr. Lee would buy (and more importantly, her receptionist who guarded the door into that mystical therapy room).

CHAPTER 5

*a*s I got into my car and started the engine, I couldn't help but feel a sense of desperation wash over me. I was on my way to Dr. Sandra Lee's office, but I wasn't going as myself - I was going as Iva Claire, the young woman whose identity I had stolen. God, I felt so bad for stealing her identity and the time slot that she'd waited months for… But I needed it more than her, or anyone.

It wasn't a decision I had made lightly. But I was desperate. I needed Dr. Lee's help again, this time to cure me of a new addiction to men that had taken hold of me. And I knew that if I went to Dr. Lee as myself, she would turn me away—if I could even get through the door before security apprehended me.

As I pulled into the parking lot of Dr. Lee's office,

I could feel my palms starting to sweat. This was it, the moment of truth. I had to go through with this, or I would never be cured of this new addiction.

I kept my head down and tried to blend in with the crowd, hoping that no one would recognize me. But every time someone looked my way, my heart would skip a beat.

I took a deep breath and got out of the car, making my way into the building.

As I walked into Dr. Sandra Lee's office, I couldn't help but feel a knot form in my stomach. I was disguised as Iva Claire, but what if someone saw through my disguise? What if Dr. Lee knew who I really was and refused to help me?

But I had to take the chance. This was my only chance to see Dr. Lee again, to beg for her help in curing me of this new addiction that had taken hold of me. I couldn't let it go any longer.

As I approached the receptionist's desk, I could feel my heart pounding in my chest. I kept my head down, hoping that no one would recognize me. But the receptionist simply looked up and smiled, and asked for my name.

"Iva Claire," I said, my voice trembling slightly. I don't even think I spoke as loud as a whisper.

The receptionist nodded and handed me a clipboard with some forms to fill out. As I took the clipboard, I couldn't help but glance around the waiting room, trying to see if anyone was staring at me. But everyone seemed to be minding their own business, lost in their own thoughts.

I quickly filled out the forms, trying to keep my hands from shaking too much. When I handed them back to the receptionist, she gave me a warm smile and told me to take a seat.

As I sat down, I felt a sense of relief wash over me. I had made it this far, and no one had recognized me yet. Maybe I could really pull this off. I was close—closer than ever before. There was hope for me... but I still didn't know what I was going to tell the doctor.

But I knew that the hard part was yet to come. I had to face Dr. Lee and beg for her help. And I had to hope that she would still be willing to help me, even though I was using a false identity.

I closed my eyes and took a deep breath, trying to calm my nerves.

As I sat in the waiting room, I couldn't help but feel like every minute was an hour. The clock on the wall seemed to tick by at an excruciatingly slow pace, mocking me with its steady rhythm. Tick, tock, tick, tock, tick....

I tried to distract myself with a magazine, flipping through the pages with a restless energy. But I couldn't focus on the words or the images - my mind was consumed with worry and fear.

What if Dr. Lee recognized me? What if she knew that I was really Owen, and not Iva Claire? What if she turned me away, refused to help me?

Every time someone walked through the door, my heart would skip a beat, and I would hold my breath, hoping that they weren't here to see Dr. Lee. But they always were, and I would sink back into my seat with a sense of defeat. And every time someone came through the door, I was partly terrified that it would be the real Iva Claire, there to expose me as a fraud and a criminal.

The minutes stretched on, seeming to go on forever. I could feel the sweat on my palms, the tightness in my chest. I wanted to get up and leave, to run away from this nightmare. But I knew that I couldn't. I needed Dr. Lee's help, and I had to see this through.

Finally, after what felt like an eternity, the receptionist called Iva's name. I stood up, feeling like my legs were made of lead, and made my way to the door. It was time to face Dr. Lee, to beg for her help, and to hope that she would be willing to give it to me.

Her office was somehow different than I remembered. There were large plants in every corner of the room. The roof seemed somehow higher, and the walls seemed tighter, as if they were closing in on me.

"Take a seat," said Dr. Lee with a smile on her face. "Let's get into it right away. I imagine you're relieved to finally be here with me."

"Yes," I said softly.

"Are you nervous?"

I shrugged my shoulders.

"Well," Dr. Lee said, as I sat down across from her in her office. "It's nice to see you again. How have you been feeling?"

I tried to keep my voice steady as I responded, doing my best to imitate Iva's soft tone. "I've been okay," I said. "But I've been struggling with some issues lately."

Dr. Lee leaned forward, looking at me with a concerned expression. "What kind of issues?" she asked. "Related to your brother again?"

I took a deep breath, and then launched into the story that I had practiced in my head a hundred times. I told her about my recent struggles with anxiety, about how I had been having panic attacks at work, and how I had been unable to sleep at night. And then, I began to segue into the real issue: the blackouts, the strange urges to seek out men.

Dr. Lee listened attentively, nodding her head in all the right places. When I was finished, she leaned back in her chair and looked at me thoughtfully.

"Well, I think I can help you with that," she said. "I've developed a new process that I think could be very effective in treating what sound like very troubling episodes. It's a form of hypnosis that I call 'reprogramming therapy.'"

She went on to explain how the process worked, how she would put me into a deep state of relaxation, and then use a series of carefully crafted suggestions to help rewire my brain, replacing negative thoughts with positive ones. It all sounded very generic, but I knew how powerful she was, so I remained optimistic. She gave me this illness, so surely she could also take it away.

"It's a very powerful technique," she said. "And I've had a lot of success with it in the past. I think it could be just what you need to overcome your episodes."

I listened to her words, feeling a sense of hope rising up within me. Maybe this was it! Maybe this was the key to curing me of my new addiction— whatever you might call it.

Now, she was staring into my eyes, with a slight grin on her face. There was a silence in the room.

"First, I'm going to lead you into a simple, relaxed state of mind. Relax into the couch. Close your eyes. Listen carefully to my words, and we'll work on clearing your mind."

"Okay," I whispered. It was hard to relax, knowing that I could slip at any moment, especially if she was going to hypnotize me. What if I ended up telling her who I really was? Would she call the police and have me arrested for identity theft?

"Good," she said, her voice soft and soothing. "Now, I want you to imagine yourself in a calm, peaceful place. Somewhere that makes you feel safe and happy. It could be a beach, a forest, a mountain-top… Anywhere that brings you a sense of serenity."

I closed my eyes, and tried to follow her instructions. I imagined myself standing on a quiet beach, with the sound of waves lapping at my feet, and a warm breeze blowing through my hair. It was peaceful and calm, and I felt myself relaxing.

"Good," Dr. Lee said, her voice a gentle whisper. "Now, I want you to focus on your breathing. Take slow, deep breaths, and feel yourself sinking deeper and deeper into relaxation."

I did as she said, taking deep breaths in and out, feeling the tension slowly melting away from my body.

"Very good," Dr. Lee said. "Now, I want you to picture a door in your mind. Do you see the door, Iva?"

"Yes," I whispered. I could see the door very

clearly, in fact, as if it was really there in front of me. There was something about Dr. Lee's words, something about the way that she spoke. It wasn't necessarily the words that she chose, but it was the tone of her voice; it almost seemed to resonate in my head, as if she was speaking directly into my ear. Dr. Lee's voice was a thing of profound intensity. It was a soft, soothing whisper that seemed to wrap around me like a warm blanket. But there was an underlying power to it as well, a sense of authority and control that commanded my attention and held it fast.

As she spoke, I felt myself slipping into a trance, my mind completely focused on her words. It was as if nothing else existed in the world; there was just me, and her voice, and the sense of calm and peace that came with it.

And yet, there was also a subtle undercurrent of danger to her voice - a sense that she could take me anywhere she wanted, and that I would have no choice but to follow. It was a feeling of vulnerability and submission that was both terrifying and exhilarating.

In that moment, I realized just how skilled Dr. Lee was as a hypnotherapist. She had a way of weaving words together that was both hypnotic and persuasive, drawing me deeper and deeper into a world of her own making. It was both thrilling and frightening at the same time, and I couldn't help but wonder what she was capable of doing with that power.

"Now, Iva, I want you to sink deeper into your state of relaxation. Can you still hear me? Are you still with me?"

"Yes," I said softly.

"Okay, good. Now, tell me your real name."

My heart fluttered. My stomach turned. Why was she asking for my real name? Was she onto me?

I wanted to lie to her, but I was incapable of lying. She had control over me. "Owen Baker," I said.

"And why did you steal Iva Claire's name and identity, Owen?" she asked with that calming voice.

My heart raced. It was a feeling that I now knew

all too well: being trapped in my own body, watching and listening as my body acted against my will. "I stole her appointment, to see you," I said, hypnotized.

"Identity theft is a crime, Owen," she said. "It's a serious crime. Do you understand the severity of what you've done?"

"Yes."

"Do you understand that I could call the police right now and have you arrested?"

"Yes."

"So what is it that you really want?" she asked.

My heart was pounding ferociously. I had no control. I wanted to get up and run, but I couldn't move a single muscle.

"Whenever I'm stressed out, I blackout."

"What happens when you blackout, Owen?"

"I become a different person. I put on a wig and women's clothing, and makeup. I go out and seduce men."

"What do you do with these men?"

"I beg them to fuck me. I beg them to let me suck them off."

"And when do these blackouts end?" she asked.

"Once I get what I want," I said bluntly.

"And this started after our appointment, did it?"

"Yes," I said.

"And you think that I did it to you, Owen?"

"Yes."

"What makes you think that?"

"It's the only possibility," I said.

"I didn't do that to you, Owen. In fact, I record all of my hypnosis sessions. Your particular session was only five minutes long, like most of my smoking cases. Would you like me to play back your session for you, so you can hear for yourself?"

I was silent, trembling all over, still wanting to get up and run out of that room before I ended up being arrested. She went to her computer and loaded up my last session. She played it. She let it run from start to finish; it really only was a few minutes long. She even played back the part where I yelled at her and accused her of being a scam artist.

"Are you still smoking?" she asked me.

"No," I said.

"Good," she said. She paused for a moment, as if considering her words carefully. "Well, Owen," she said, her voice soft and soothing. "It's possible that your addiction to smoking was simply a mask, a way of hiding from something deeper and more profound. Something that you may not even be fully aware of yet."

She leaned forward in her chair, her gaze fixed on mine. "It's not uncommon for people to use vices like smoking as a way of numbing themselves to difficult emotions. But when we take away that crutch, those emotions can come rushing to the surface. And sometimes, they can take unexpected forms."

I felt a sense of panic rising inside of me. Was she suggesting that I was gay? That I was some kind of pervert? Was she suggesting that I secretly loved going out and finding men to fuck my brains out?

But Dr. Lee seemed to sense my discomfort. "Don't be afraid, Owen," she said, her voice soothing. "There's nothing wrong with who you are. We all have different desires and urges - it's what makes us human. And if exploring these urges is what you need to do to find happiness and peace, then that's what we'll work on."

She leaned back in her chair, a small smile playing at the corner of her lips. "But for now," she said, her voice slipping back into that hypnotic whisper. "I want you to focus on the present. On this moment, and the possibilities that lie before you."

As Dr. Lee's words echoed through my mind, I felt a terrible sense of panic rising up inside of me.

Could it be true?

Was I gay?

The thought was terrifying... not because I had anything against gay people, but because it would mean that everything I thought I knew about myself was wrong.

For as long as I could remember, I had been attracted to women. I had dated plenty of them, and had never even considered the possibility that I might be interested in men. But now, with Dr. Lee's words ringing in my ears, I couldn't shake the feeling that there was something inside of me that I had been ignoring... something that I didn't want to face.

No! It was impossible. I wasn't attracted to men. Even now, as I sat in that office, I could muster up the image of a woman in my mind and get a certain satisfaction from it—a satisfaction that I couldn't get from thinking about a man. I loved the idea of being with a woman, romantically. I loved everything about women: their curves, their soft hair, their delicate nature. In fact, I loved women so much that I couldn't help but love the idea of being one myself...

I froze up suddenly as that thought entered my brain. I allowed it to resonate for a moment, even though I badly wanted to chase it away. Was that thought my own, or was it implanted in me by the hypnotherapist?

Now, I was thinking about men again, but not in a romantic sense. I wasn't romantically interested in men... but I did enjoy the thought of being dominated by them. I thought back on all of the sexual experiences that I could remember with men, over the past couple of months. I let out a soft whimper, remembering the intense satisfaction of being used by a horny man: being pumped and filled... It was a terrifying thought. But at the same time, there was a part of me that felt a strange sense of excitement at the thought. A part of me that had always been curious about what it would be like to be with a man, even though I had never acted on it consciously.

As I sat there in Dr. Lee's office, I felt like I was on the edge of a precipice, looking out into an uncertain future. But one thing was certain - things would never be the same again.

Dr. Lee studied me for a moment, as if weighing her words carefully. "Owen, I believe that you may be experiencing what we call gender dysphoria. It's a condition where a person's gender identity doesn't match the sex they were assigned at birth. It's a complex issue, and one that can be difficult to come to terms with."

I felt a sense of shock wash over me. Was she suggesting that I was transgender? The thought was somehow both terrifying and exhilarating. Could it be possible that all of these confusing feelings and urges that I had been experiencing were simply the result of being born into the wrong body?

But before I could even begin to process what she was saying, Dr. Lee continued. "It's also possible that you're bisexual - that you're attracted to both men and women. These are both valid identities, Owen, and ones that we can work on exploring together."

As I sat there, stunned and uncertain, Dr. Lee's words echoed through my mind. Could it be possible that I was both transgender and bisexual? It was a lot to take in, to say the least.

Dr. Lee's voice was soft and gentle as she spoke, but her words hit me like a ton of bricks. "Owen, I believe that you stole Iva's identity because, deep down, you wanted to be a girl like her. You were drawn to her, and to the life that she lived, because it represented something that you were craving: a chance to be someone else, someone different."

I felt a sense of shame wash over me as I heard her words. Was it true? Had I really been so desperate to escape myself that I had resorted to stealing someone else's identity? It was a painful thought, but at the same time, there was a strange sense of relief in it, like I was finally starting to understand what was going on inside of me.

Dr. Lee leaned forward in her chair, her gaze fixed on mine. "But Owen," she said, her voice soft but firm. "You can't run from who you are. You can't escape your own identity, no matter how hard you try. And in the end, it will only lead to more pain and confusion. It's possible that when we took the crutch of smoking away from you, your body no longer had a coping mechanism to hide from your deepest feelings and desires, so it started to manifest a second identity."

I felt sick, but still frozen, still unable to move from the spot where I was hypnotized. She still had control over me. And it seemed like she was still trying to decide what to do with me.

"Owen, when I snap my fingers you will regain control of yourself. But first, I want you to imagine a doorway, in your mind. I want you to slowly approach this doorway. On the other side of the door is your true self: the person you want to be more than anything else in the world. And on the other side of that door, there is no judgement: no self-judgement and no judgement from others. Once you're on the other side of that door, you can be whoever you want to be, whether that's a man, a woman, a homosexual, a bisexual, or a heterosexual. Step through that doorway."

I did as she asked, feeling a shockwave of warm

energy flowing through me. Then, she snapped her fingers. I suddenly felt control returning to me. I looked into her eyes, seeing that she was watching me closely with that dark grin.

"You—You're not going to call the cops, are you?" I asked.

She laughed, shook her head, and then she pointed at the door. "You have thirty seconds to get out of this building before I call the police." Her demeanour had changed completely. Her tone of voice was no longer soothing or hypnotic. Now, she clearly remembered the way I spoke to her after our last session.

I scurried out of her office, past her receptionist, and I headed straight to my car, heart pounding. The rest of that day was filled with uncertainty, worried that the police were going to show up at my door at any moment.

I sat on the edge of the bathtub in my small bathroom, staring at my reflection in the mirror. It was like I was seeing myself for the first time... or at least, seeing a part of myself that I had never really acknowledged before. I was still dressed like Iva, still with those fake freckles and that reddened nose.

Dr. Lee's words echoed through my mind - about being transgender, about being bisexual, about stealing Iva's identity because I wanted to be a girl like her. It was all so much to take in, and I didn't even know where to begin.

But as I sat there, my mind racing with thoughts and questions, a part of me felt like a weight had been lifted. Like maybe, just maybe, there was a reason for all of the confusion and pain that I had been feeling.

I looked down at my hands, still shaking with emotion. I spent a minute trying to collect myself, trying to catch my breath. I could feel a lightheadedness coming on, and I wondered if it was going to end with one of those blackout episodes.

I took a deep breath, steadying myself, and began to remove the makeup that I had put on earlier. As I wiped away the last traces of foundation and mascara, I felt strange, like I was washing away a piece of me. Without the makeup there, I just felt... bare. It felt like something was wrong and out of place.

I looked back up at myself in the mirror, feeling a strange sense of anticipation. There was a whole world of possibility out there, and for the first time in a long time, I felt like maybe, just maybe, I was ready to start exploring it.

I grabbed my makeup and put a touch of mascara back on, and suddenly that lightheadedness fluttered away. An intense satisfaction filled me and then the muscles in my tense body seemed to relax all at once. I let out a soft sigh of relief. The feeling only got better when I retrieved a gentle piece of lingerie to put over my skin.

It felt good, but it wasn't quite appropriate to wear out. This time, I wasn't going out to find some easy target; I wasn't going out to find a man who could fuck my brains out and satisfy deep-down desires that had been festering for years—maybe even decades.

I rummaged through the box of dresses and skirts, trying to find the perfect outfit for the night. I had already put on my makeup and styled my hair, feeling more beautiful than I ever had before. It was like something inside me had clicked into place, and for the first time, I felt like the person I had always been meant to be.

As I tried on different clothes, I pondered different names for my new identity. Iva had been a good name, but it didn't feel like me. Maybe something more classic, like Elizabeth or Victoria. Or something more modern, like Madison or Peyton.

The excitement was growing by the second. I couldn't stop smiling. I tried biting my lip to keep the smile away, but it didn't help much.

I settled on Madison, liking the way it sounded when I whispered it to myself. It felt like a fresh start, a chance to be someone new, someone better.

I slipped on a tight-fitting dress and admired myself in the mirror. It hugged my curves in all the right places, and I couldn't help but feel a surge of excitement. It was like I was a new person, free to explore a whole new world of possibility. Oh God, that fabric was so amazingly soft on my skin; that feeling alone made all of this uncertainty worthwhile.

As I stepped outside, the cool night air sending shivers down my spine, I felt a sense of fear and excitement wash over me. I was scared of what people might say or think, but at the same time, I was excited to show off my new self to the world. Dr. Lee gave me this gift, whether or not I deserved it.

And as I walked down the street, feeling the eyes of strangers on me, I knew that this was just the beginning of my new life as Madison. A life that was beautiful, exciting, and full of endless possibility.

THE END

FIND ME ON PATREON!

I really hope that you're enjoying my work! I've been fortunate enough to make this my full-time job for the past couple of years, though it hasn't been easy. There's a lot of financial uncertainty as a full-time self-published writer.

I would feel tremendously blessed if you would venture on over to my Patreon page and consider supporting me there. I think you will be excited by what I have to offer: **a community, free book chapters, pictures, contests, commissions, free stories, advanced releases, and much more**. It's the only way to get your hands on these exclusive titles:

THE PUNISHMENT
FORCED

TWINS
LORI'S LAST FUCK
THE GIRL TWIN (A Full-Length Novel)
TRANS CAM WHORE
GETTING READY FOR PROM
DUBIOUS CONSENT
PETRA'S FRISKY PHOTOSHOOT
JILLIAN'S 14 INCHES
THREE WISHES
HIS BIGGEST FAN
TRUTH OR DARE
ONLY GIRLS GET A RIDE
WEREWOMAN

And for as little as a dollar per month—is that even a quarter cup of Starbucks coffee?
Be the gorgeous, filthy doll you know that you are and come hang out with me:

https://www.patreon.com/nikkicrescent

NEWSLETTER

JOIN NIKKI CRESCENT'S MAILING LIST!

Thank you for picking up one of my books! Chances are I'm in the process of working on another one! Hey—Did you know that you can read my whole catalogue free if you subscribe to **Kindle Unlimited**? It's true! If you aren't subscribed, I would highly recommend it.

I have started this little newsletter to let all of my beautiful readers know when I'm offering discounts, releasing new books, and giving away **EXCLUSIVE CONTENT FOR FREE**. The sign up takes about four seconds (seriously). I will never share your email address with anyone, you will never receive any spam, and you can unsubscribe at any time with the click of a single button.

CLICK HERE TO SIGN UP FOR NIKKI CRESCENT'S MAILING LIST NOW!

Can't open the link? Copy and paste this link into your browser:

http://eepurl.com/O3CKz

ABOUT THE AUTHOR

NIKKI CRESCENT

Nikki Crescent is a young writer from the golden prairies of Alberta, Canada. She spent her schooling years lost in her own imagination, writing everything from articles, screenplays, comic books, and short stories. Obsessed with the idea of love, fascinated with sex and captivated with the art of writing, Nikki decided to become a writer of erotic romance.

Nikki Crescent is a top-selling writer of romantic and erotic fiction with over two hundred and fifty titles across many sub-genres. Her fiction work has found her on Amazon's best-selling charts many times over.

93223911R00090